THIS WALKER BOOK BELONGS TO:

_____

_____

_____

_____

For Finbar
and Jock

First published 1994 by Walker Books Ltd
87 Vauxhall Walk, London SE11 5HJ

This edition published 1995

10 9 8 7 6 5 4 3 2 1

© 1994 Flora McDonnell

This book has been typeset in New Baskerville.

Printed in Hong Kong

British Library Cataloguing
in Publication Data
A catalogue record for this book is
available from the British Library.

ISBN 0-7445-4346-0

I Love Animals

Flora McDonnell

WALKER BOOKS

AND SUBSIDIARIES

LONDON • BOSTON • SYDNEY

I love Jock, my dog.

I love
the ducks

waddling to
the water.

I love the hens
hopping up
and down.

I love the goat

racing across
the field.

I love the donkey

braying
"hee-haw!"

I love the cow swishing her tail.

I love the pig with

all her little piglets.

I love the pony

rolling

over

and

over.

I love the sheep
bleating to
her lamb.

I love
the cat

washing her
kittens.

I love the turkey

strutting
round
the yard.

I love all
the animals.

I hope they love me.

MORE WALKER PAPERBACKS
For You to Enjoy

NOISY NOISES ON THE FARM
by Julie Lacome

Animal sounds, colourful pictures and a delightful conclusion make this story of a cat looking for a quiet place on the farm a thoroughly enjoyable picture book for young children.

0-7445-2336-2   £2.99

ANIMAL ALPHABET / ANIMAL NUMBERS
by Bert Kitchen

Two concept books of stunning animal paintings.

"Very beautiful... In the category of 'collectable classics'... As much for adults as for children." *Books for Keeps*

Animal Alphabet   0-7445-1776-1
Animal Numbers   0-7445-1780-X
£4.99 each

KENNETH LILLY'S ANIMALS
by Kenneth Lilly

A magnificent collection of animal portraits by one of this country's finest naturalist artists, arranged according to habitat, with an authoritative text by Joyce Pope, formerly of the Natural History Museum.

"Every page opening is a pleasure ... made memorable by Lilly's outstanding illustrations. A book not just for a summer holiday but for a lifetime." *The Independent*

0-7445-2356-7   £7.99